Published by Caroline House
Boyds Mills Press, Inc.
A Highlights Company
815 Church Street
Honesdale, Pennsylvania 18431
Printed in China

U.S. Cataloging-in-Publication Data
  (Library of Congress Standards)

Gibbons, Faye.
    Emma Jo's song / by Faye Gibbons ; illustrated by
Sherry Meidell.—1st ed.
[32]p. : col. ill. ; cm.
Summary: Emma musters the courage to sing in public when
she's joined by an old hound dog.
ISBN 1-56397-935-7
1. Singing—Fiction. I. Meidell, Sherry, ill. II. Title.
  [E] 21 2001 AC   CIP
00-101647

First edition, 2001
The text of this book is set in 13-point Stone Serif.

10 9 8 7 6 5 4 3 2 1

Visit our Web site at
www.boydsmillspress.com

For my daughter-in-law,
Laurie McNabb Gibbons,
who has many gifts.
—F. G.

For my friend Shannon Sutton—guitar picker.

—S.M.

3

The corn was just coming in and the watermelons were getting ripe when we went to the Puckett family reunion. We all jumped out of bed soon as the rooster crowed on that fine day. Seemed like everybody but me was making music.

Pa sang while he milked cows, and my big brother, Tom, yodeled while he slopped the hogs. My little brothers, Lenny and Sam, whistled while fetching wood. Mama hummed while she cooked breakfast, and my sister, Helen, sang while she toted water from the spring.

Me, I kept quiet even though a song was just bustin' to get out of me. I wasn't good at music and singing like the rest of them. Grandpa always said I had a gift, but I hadn't found it yet.

"Emma Jo, feed the chickens," Mama called,
and I lit out for the barn lot. While I scattered corn,
I commenced to sing real low. "This little light of mine, I'm gonna
let it shine. . . ."

Just my luck—that ol' hound dog of ours heard me.

"*O-o-o-o-o-o-o!*" he howled, and came galloping from the hogpen with
his nose pointed straight up. "*O-o-o-o-o-o-o!*"

Tom came right behind him, whooping with laughter. I flew mad.

"That dog's not going with us to the reunion!" I yelled.

Tom stopped laughing. "Just because he likes to sing 'This Little Light
of Mine' with you?"

"Rip howls with everything I sing," I answered.

"Aw, come on with me, Rip," Tom called.

The sky was glowing pink beyond the Georgia mountains when we loaded dinner into the wagon. Pa put on his best straw hat and helped Mama up on the wagon seat.

"You taking your harmonica?" she asked. Pa patted his shirt pocket, and Mama said, "Good. I'm taking my dulcimer, too."

Helen laid her songbook in the wagon, and Tom ran out of the house swinging his fiddle. Still whistling, Lenny and Sam followed close behind. Rip danced around our legs.

"Needn't set in to begging," I told him. "You ain't going."

"He is so," said Tom.

Pa looked at Tom and then at me. "Well," he finally said, "I reckon a dog's got no business at a family reunion."

"That's right," I said.

Pa pointed a finger at Rip. "Stay."

Rip dropped to the ground, but when the wagon began to rumble away, he lifted his head and let out a howl.

I felt mean.

The howling followed us past the garden and cornfield, between the orchard and pasture, over the creek, and through the woods. It didn't stop until we pulled onto County Road Six.

11

We heard the music and the singing a long way off. "Shall we gather at the river?" the kinfolk sang, and I felt it to my bones. When Pa turned off the highway onto Talking Rock River Road, the relatives started on "Wildwood Flower." Pa and Mama joined in, and so did Tom, Helen, Lenny, and Sam. Inside my head, I sang, too.

Then a big white house came into sight. The talking and the singing, the guitar strumming and the piano plinking, the wailing of a harmonica, and the picking of a banjo came to meet us.

There were Pucketts everywhere. Pucketts in the rockers on the front porch, Pucketts in the clean-swept yard, Pucketts out under the trees and setting up makeshift tables in the shade. There were Pucketts talking and hugging, Pucketts laughing and crying. But best of all, there were Pucketts singing and making all kinds of music.

While the music swirled around me, I played with all the cousins. We waded in the creek and swung on wild grapevines. We climbed in the barn loft and slid on the hay. We played hide-and-seek and pop-the-whip until it was time to go into the house.

The parlor was crowded and hot, and soon every chair was filled.
Pucketts stood up around the walls and spread out into the big hallway.
I sat on the floor between Grandpa Puckett and my brother Tom.
Grandpa was dozing, making little whistle-snorts into his beard.

Funeral-home fans stirred the air while groups of two and three and
four sang along with piano, guitar, and fiddle. There were solos, too.
Helen sang two of them. Grandpa snored through every one.

Finally, one of the uncles asked for one last song before dinner.

"*Snork-k-k-k-k-k!*" went Grandpa, slumping to one side of his chair.

Tom grinned at me. "Emma Jo could sing 'This Little Light of Mine,'" he said.

I wasn't going to let him tease me. I jumped up before I had time to think. "All right, I will."

Tom's smile was gone in a flash. He got up and plunked himself down on the piano stool. "Reckon I'll play for you," he said.

"You will?" I said, surprised and glad.

Tom nodded and began to play.

I looked around at all those Pucketts, and my knees got weak.
I opened my mouth and . . .

"*Snork-wheeeeeeeeee!*" went Grandpa.

Everyone laughed and Tom began again. My voice was a quivering squeak. "This little light of mine, I'm gonna let it shine. . . ."

Several of the cousins giggled, and my voice wandered away from the tune. Tom played louder.

"This little light of mine," I sang on, squeaking even more.
Suddenly there came a clawing outside the window next to
me and then a mournful whine. Then there were two white
paws on the window ledge, and between them a black nose.

"It's Rip!" Tom whispered, just as that good-for-nothing
hound pulled himself through the window.

I made myself sing on, "I'm gonna let it shine. . . ."

"*O-o-o-o-o-o-o*" Rip howled, leaping to the floor beside me
and pointing his nose to the ceiling. "*O-o-o-o-o-o-o!*"

24.

Grandpa woke with a snort and almost toppled from his chair.
I made my voice louder. "This little light of mine, . . ."
Suddenly Tom's voice blended with mine. "I'm gonna let it shine."
Helen leaped up to stand beside me and joined in the song. "Let it shine, let it shine, let it shine!"

Rip howled louder, and then Lenny and Sam stood up. Then we were all standing and singing together, and suddenly my voice sounded strong. We all sounded good together.

When we finished, Rip gave one last howl and the whole room pure exploded. Aunts and uncles and cousins were all laughing and clapping together.

Grandpa jumped to his feet. "Now that was good!" he said. "Who trained that dog?"

"Emma Jo," Tom answered, patting Rip on the head.

Grandpa grinned and slapped his knee. "That girl's got a gift. Didn't I always say so?"

In a little while everybody was outside, gathering around the tables. I filled a plate with fried chicken, creamed corn, and apple pie. Then I fixed Rip a plate.